Hello boys and girls let's talk about Thanksgiving which is an important holiday in America

2022 ♡ mimi x PopPop

on this day we watch parades decorate
our houses and have a big family dinner

but do you know where this holiday
came from let's learn more about
the first Thanksgiving Day

In 1620, Pilgrims crossed the Atlantic Ocean on a huge ship.

They wanted to start

their new life in America

But they had arrived in

the peak of winter

The first winter was very
difficult

it was a tough cold winter and they did not have enough food, many people got very sick

when the spring came the
pilgrims had to learn how to
feed themselves

They didn't know how to farm or hunt.

The native Americans showed
them how to grow plants
such as corn

The native American were a
great farmers

They were the people who had long lived in America they knew how to survive and grow food on this land in the fall the pilgrims gathered a big harvest

this means that they had

plenty of food to eat

they decided to have a fancy dinner
they're native American neighbors
were invited to the celebration

the pilgrims were thankful that they
had settle in a new place and started a
new life.

since that Americans come together on thanksgiving to celebrate the things that they are thankful for family, food, shelter and

good health, are just

few things that many

people give thanks for

this day.

Made in United States
North Haven, CT
21 November 2022